A MERIT BADGE MYSTERY™

The Berenstain BEAR SCOUTS
AND THE
STINKY MILK MYSTERY

ISBN 0-590-56524-9

Copyright © 1999 by Berenstain Enterprises, Inc.
All rights reserved. Published by Scholastic Inc.
SCHOLASTIC, CARTWHEEL BOOKS and associated logos
are trademarks and/or registered trademarks of Scholastic Inc.
Merit Badge Mystery is a registered trademark of Berenstain Enterprises.

Library of Congress Cataloging-in-Publication Data available

LC: 98-41400

12 11 10 9 8 7 6 5 4 3 2 1   9/9 0/0 01 02 03

Printed in the U.S.A.   24
First printing, April 1999

The Berenstain BEAR SCOUTS

AND THE
STINKY MILK MYSTERY

Stan & Jan Berenstain

Illustrated by Michael Berenstain

Cartwheel B·O·O·K·S ®

SCHOLASTIC INC.

New York   Toronto   London   Auckland   Sydney

The Bear Scouts were bored. They were sitting around their clubhouse trying to figure out what to do. Scout Sister was reading the Bear Scout Handbook.

"Let's earn another merit badge," she said. "We haven't gotten the Popsicle Stick Craft Merit Badge, yet."

"Oh, boy," said Scout Brother, yawning, "I can hardly wait."

Scout Lizzy was looking out of the window. "What's Farmer Ben doing over there?" she asked.

Farmer Ben was hard at work fixing his pasture fence.

"It looks like Farmer Ben could use some help," said Scout Fred.

"Bear Scouts are always helpful," said Brother.

"And Farmer Ben is our neighbor," added Lizzy.

"<u>And</u>…," said Sister, holding up the Scout Handbook, "we can earn the Good Neighbor Merit Badge."

The Bear Scouts were out of the clubhouse in a flash and heading for Farmer Ben's fence.

"Farmer Ben! Farmer Ben!" they called. "Do you need some help?"

"Why, thank you, kindly!" said Farmer
Ben, wiping his forehead with his kerchief.
"That's very neighborly of you."

"What should we do?" asked Sister.

"Well, now," said Farmer Ben, "you see
where those cows of mine have strayed
through the broken fence into the next field?"

They all looked and nodded.

"If you could round 'em up and shoo 'em
back into my pasture," said Ben, "I could
finish fixing the fence."

This job was just right for the Bear Scouts. Waving their hats and shouting, "YEE-HA!" they quickly rounded up the cows and chased them back into the pasture where they belonged.

"That's fine," said Farmer Ben. "Now,
just one more rail." The Scouts helped lift
it in place. "And we're done!"

"What's next?" asked Scout Sister.
This was more fun than sitting around the
clubhouse trying to figure out what to do.

"Well," said Ben, "if you really want to help, there are always chores to be done around the farm."

And so, the Bear Scouts went to work.

They fed the chickens.

They collected the eggs.

They slopped the hogs

and they cleaned out the barn.

Soon, they were tired and covered
with bits of straw. But there was still
more work to be done. Sitting around
the clubhouse doing nothing was
starting to look a lot better.

"It's almost milking time," said
Farmer Ben. "Let's call the cows into
the barn."

"Here, Bossie! Here, Bossie!" the Scouts called with Farmer Ben.

The cows all herded into the barn
and lined up in their stalls.

Farmer Ben went from cow to cow with a milk pail and a stool and milked the cows. He showed the Bear Scouts how to do it. Farmer Ben was an expert. He could squirt milk right into the barn cats' mouths.

But wait a minute!

Why were the cats making faces and spitting out the milk? Was there something wrong with it?

Scout Sister took a taste.

YUCK!

It was stinky! It tasted sour and smelled bad! "What in the world happened to my milk?" gasped Farmer Ben. "It's never tasted like this before!"

It was a mystery — the stinky milk mystery!

That's when Scout Lizzy noticed that Dr. Wise Old Owl had been asleep in the rafters of the barn. Maybe *he* would be able to solve the stinky milk mystery.

"Dr. Wise Old Owl! Dr. Wise Old Owl!" called Lizzy, "Can you tell us why Farmer Ben's milk turned bad?"

"What does that mean?" wondered Scout Sister. "The green on the other side of *what?*"

"Of the fence!" answered Scout Fred. "The grass is always greener on the other side of the fence."

"Hmmm!" said Scout Brother. "Maybe we should take a look at the other side of that fence."

So, the Scouts and Farmer Ben went out to the pasture and climbed over the fence into the next field.

Scout Lizzy pulled up a clump of grass. There was a stinky smell. "Look!" she said, wrinkling her nose. "Onion grass!"

"Onion grass!" said Farmer Ben. "So, that's what happened! My cows strayed through the broken fence and ate some onion grass that turned their milk sour."

And that was, indeed, what had happened.

The Bear Scouts had earned their Good Neighbor Merit Badge.

But what about the spoiled milk? Farmer Ben was afraid they would have to throw it all out.

Then, Mrs. Ben had a wonderful idea. She made a huge batch of cream of onion soup.

It was delicious!